P9-DUD-557

MIGHTY READER

AND THE READING RIDDLE

Will Hillenbrand

HOLIDAY HOUSE · NEW YORK

To Pabby Arnold, a magical librarian.

Text and illustrations copyright © 2022 by Will Hillenbrand
All rights reserved.
HOLIDAY HOUSE is reigstered in the U.S. Patent and Trademark Office
Printed and bound in March 2022 at Toppan Leefung, DongGuan, China.
The artwork was created digitally with Adobe Fresco.
www.holidayhouse.com
First Edition
1 3 5 7 9 10 8 6 4 2
Library of Congress Cataloging-in-Publication Data is available.

ISBN 978-0-8234-4500-4 (hardcover)

Inky rushed from intervention to the library.

ACTION ADVENTURE GRAPHIC NOVEL

Try this section.

Hugo slipped behind
a display and changed into . . .

Mighty Reader!

Try this book,
The Sword
and the Bone.
It's a classic.

Mighty Reader pulled Inky into an adventure.

On the other side of the door
was a different world.

The bone bucked. Inky flew and flipped. SPLAT!

The spell book's pages were blank.

Together (with the POWER of seesaw reading), they read a grim message.

Merlin is locked in my castle dungeon. He has no books. Without anything to read, his mind will shrivel and die. Give me THE SWORD and save his miserable life.

With affection,
Smaugly the dragon

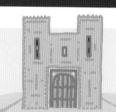

Hang on, Merlin! We are on the way.

The first plank goes diagonally across the corner.

Place the end of the second plank in the middle of the first while lowering it to the opposite bank, making a "T" bridge.

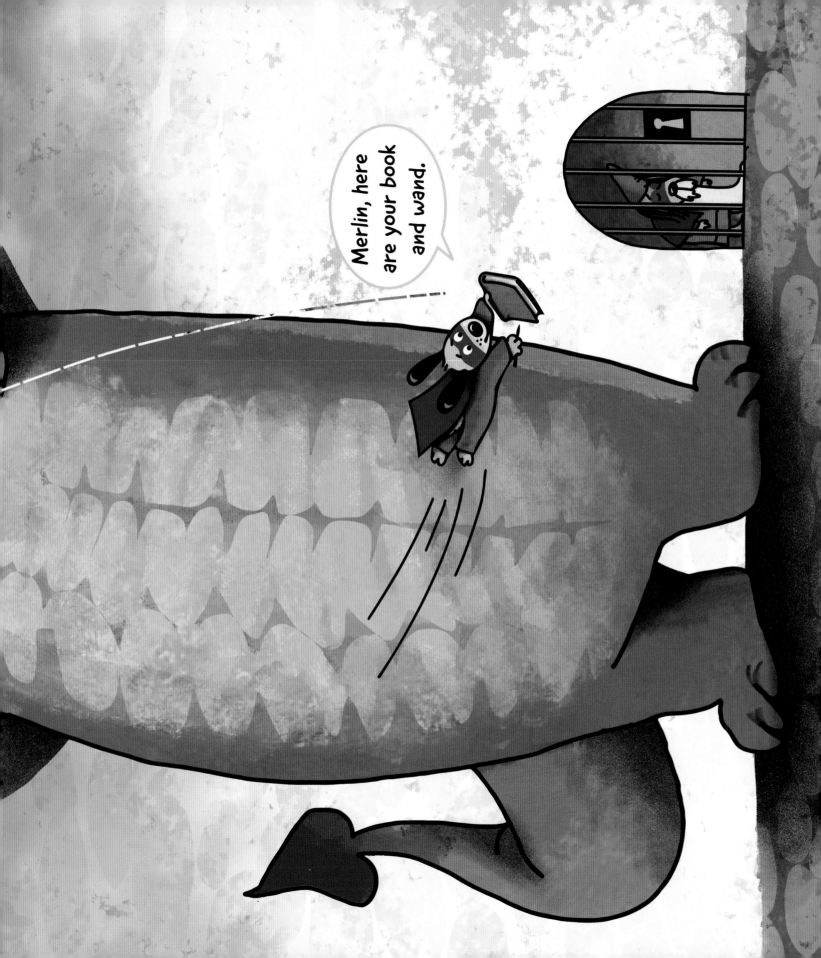

Later that night . . .

Inky couldn't wait to start reading *The Sword and the Bone*. When he opened it, he found a bookmark.

"Books are better than GOLD!"

Smaugly

The Sword and the Bone